To do LiST
- ✗ EAT porridge
- ✗ Fix CHAIR
- ✗ Eat More porridge
- ✗ MakE Bed
- 5 EAT even MoRE porridge
- 6 go FoR a nice Big WALK.

For **ELLiot**

the

newest

Little

BEAR

in

TOWN.

JuMBo OATS

honey

First published 2012 by Nosy Crow Ltd
The Crow's Nest, 10a Lant Street,
London SE1 1QR
www.nosycrow.com

ISBN 978 0 85763 043 8 (HB)
ISBN 978 0 85763 044 5 (PB)

Nosy Crow and associated logos are trademarks
and/or registered trademarks of Nosy Crow Ltd.

Copyright © Leigh Hodgkinson 2012
The right of Leigh Hodgkinson to be identified as the author
and the illustrator of this work has been asserted.

A CIP catalogue record for this book is available from the British Library.

Printed in China

3 5 7 9 10 8 6 4 2 (HB)
1 3 5 7 9 10 8 6 4 2 (PB)

Goldilocks

AND JUST THE ONE BEAR

Leigh
HODGKINSON

nosy crow

Once upon a time, there was this bear.

One minute, he was lolloping about in the wood all happy-go-lucky . . .

The next minute, he hadn't a crumb-of-a-clue where he was.

He was one  COMPLETELY lost bear.

The bear didn't much like this place.
Too many ¡BRIGHT¡ ¡Lights¡ and not enough twigs.

Too much loud HONKING and BEEPING
and not NEARLY enough owl-hooting.

The bear was also a teeny bit scared
and his furry legs had gone slightly WOBBLY.

"Maybe the thing to do," said the bear looking
round, "is to nip into 'Snooty Towers' here, and
get away from this TERRIBLE racket."

But the spinny 'Snooty Towers' door made the bear feel dizzy, and being dizzy with **WOBBLY** legs was bad news.

What the bear needed was a little sit-down.

A little sit-down somewhere would **DEFINITELY** see him tickety-boo.

level**18**

level**17**

level**16**

level**15**

level**14**

The bear peeked through a door and thought how <u>VERY</u> pleasant it was up here.

"Not nasty and <u>NOISY</u> like down there," thought the bear. "Just the place for a little sit-down."

All that **whooSHY** travelling was certainly a hungry business so, before his little sit-down, a spot of porridge seemed a good idea . . .

"THIS porridge is a bit on the D R Y side," said the bear, "but it is better than nothing."

Now the bear was ready for his little sit-down.

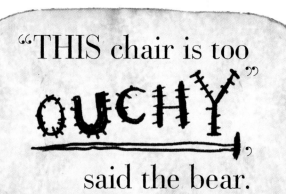

"THIS chair is JUST right!"
said the bear.

A little sit-down is all very well,
but what the bear needed to feel really tickety-boo
was a good old-fashioned lie-down in a comfy bed . . .

The bear dreamt of . . .

HOOT HOOT
HOOT

. . . CRUNCHING
through leaves.

The bear dreamt of p o t t e r i n g about in his slippers.

The bear dreamt of . . .

. . . a voice shouting very, **VERY LOUDLY.**

"**SOMEBODY** has been eating from MY fish bowl!" said the daddy person.

"Somebody has been eating MY dear little Pumpkin's kittynibbles!" said the mummy person.

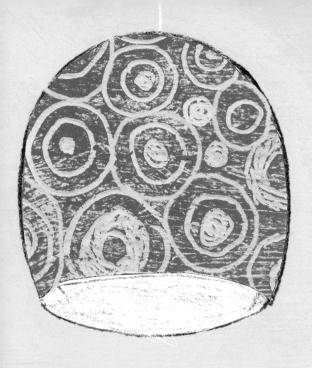

Unfortunately,
the bear was not
dreaming at all.
He was

WIDE-AWAKE

and back in real life again.

"And <u>somebody</u>
has been eating
MY toast," said
the little person.
"And they've
eaten it all up!"

"SOMEBODY has SQUISHED MY cactus!" said the daddy person.

"Somebody has UPSET MY dear little Pumpkin!" said the mummy person.

"And SOMEBODY has POPPED MY bean bag!" said the little person.

"SOMEBODY has been sleeping in MY bath!" said the daddy person.

"Somebody has been sleeping in MY bed!" said the mummy person.

"Shhhhh!" whispered the little person.
"I think THAT somebody is sleeping in
MY bed right now!"

The bear peeked from under the duvet to see a daddy person,
a mummy person and a little person standing right there.

The bear thought that the mummy person looked ever-so slightly familiar. And the mummy person thought that . . .

SCOFFING other people's breakfast,

BREAKING other people's stuff,

and **snoozing** in other people's beds . . .

seemed ever-so slightly familiar too. Then, the penny dropped . . .

"Little Bear?"

said the
mummy person.

"Goldilocks?" said the bear.

"Porridge?" asked Goldilocks.
The bear nodded.
So Goldilocks cooked up a
BIG bowl and plonked it in
front of him.

It was not too **HOT**.

It was not too **COLD**.

It was **JUST** right.

It made the bear almost forget about that once-upon-a-time when *Goldilocks* had behaved so <u>BADLY</u>.

THIS little bear would never **DREAM** of doing **ANYTHING** like that.

And although it had been good
to see Goldilocks living so *happily ever after*
with those C H A R M I N G people,
the bear decided it was time to go back
home to the woods.